SPLA

For Ted — J.O'C.

To my favorite Splat Master...
Nicky — M.M.

ISBN 0-590-62195-5

Text copyright © 1994 by Jane O'Connor.
Illustrations copyright © 1994 by Marilyn Mets.
All rights reserved. Published by Scholastic Inc., 555 Broadway, New York, NY 10012, by arrangement with Grosset & Dunlap, a member of The Putnam & Grosset Group.

12 11 10 9 8 7 6 5 4 3 2   6 7 8 9/9 0 1/0

Printed in the U.S.A.   23

First Scholastic printing, April 1996

ALL
ABOARD
READING™

**Level 1
Preschool-Grade 1**

SPLAT!

By Jane O'Connor
Illustrated by Marilyn Mets

Scholastic Inc.

New York   Toronto   London   Auckland   Sydney

I am short for my age.

And I am kind of a wimp.

My brother calls me Squirt.

But I do not want
to be Squirt anymore.
I have a plan.
I take my money
from my piggy bank.

I go to the toy store.

I see a new
Mega-Star Spaceship.
It glows in the dark.
And it flies.
But that is not
for me.

I see Crazy World.

It is the best video game.

It is in 3-D.

But that is not for me.

Then I see it—
the Drencher 1000.
There are three tanks
and a hose.
It squirts water—
lots of water.
This is for me!

DOUBLE DRENCHER 1000

DOUBLE DRENCHER 1000

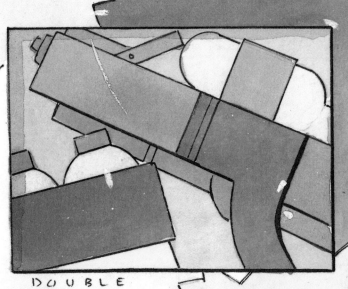

DOUBLE DRENCHER 1000

I give all my money.

And I go home.

Now I am not Squirt.

I am—

the Splat Master!

Splat!

I save good guys.

Splat!
I get bad
guys.

17

This is fun!

I start splatting everybody.

I splat my mom.

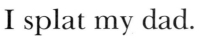
I splat my dad.

I splat my brother.

Then I run—fast!

Who else can I splat?

I see a kid.

SPLAT!

He turns around.

Uh-oh!

He has a Drencher 1000, too!

He splats me back.

I run away.

OOPS!

I fall and skin my leg.

I try not to cry.

But I do.

What a wimp!

I am not the Splat Master.

I am still just Squirt.

"I did not mean to hurt you,"
the kid tells me.
"My sister calls me PeeWee.
But my real name is Donny.
I like that better."
Donny and I become buddies.
We only splat each other
if we both say yes.
We shake on it.

Now we splat cars...

the grass...

and only sometimes
each other.
Then he is Water Man.
And I am the Splat Master.

The rest of the time
I am Tim.